My Tooth
Is Loose!

PUFFIN BOOKS
Published by the Penguin Group
Penguin Books USA Inc., 375 Hudson Street, New York, New York 10014, U.S.A.
Penguin Books Ltd, 27 Wrights Lane, London W8 5TZ, England
Penguin Books Australia Ltd, Ringwood, Victoria, Australia
Penguin Books Canada Ltd, 10 Alcorn Avenue, Toronto, Ontario, Canada M4V 3B2
Penguin Books (N.Z.) Ltd, 182-190 Wairau Road, Auckland 10, New Zealand

Penguin Books Ltd, Registered Offices: Harmondsworth, Middlesex, England

First published in the United States of America by Viking Penguin,
a division of Penguin Books USA Inc., 1992
Simultaneously published in Puffin Books
Published in a Puffin Easy-to-Read edition, 1994

13 14 15 16 17 18 19 20

Text copyright © Martin Silverman, 1992
Illustrations copyright © Amy Aitken, 1992
All rights reserved

The Library of Congress has cataloged the Viking Penguin edition under the catalog card number 90-53548.
Puffin Easy-to-Read ISBN 0-14-037001-3

Puffin® and Easy-to-Read® are registered trademarks of Penguin Books USA Inc.

Printed in the United States of America

Reading Level 1.8

My Tooth Is Loose!

Martin Silverman
Pictures by Amy Aitken

PUFFIN BOOKS

Georgie wasn't playing.
He just sat there.

"What's wrong?" asked Daniel.

"My tooth is loose," Georgie said.
"I don't know what to do!"

"When my tooth was loose,"
Daniel said, "my daddy
took it out with a string."

"I don't want a string!" said Georgie.

Then Diana came.
"What's wrong?" she asked.

"My tooth is loose," Georgie said.
"I don't know what to do."

"Bite into an apple,"
 said Diana,
"and your tooth will come out."

"I don't want to bite an apple," said Georgie.
"It might hurt!"

Then Carol came.
"What's wrong?" she asked.

"My tooth is loose," Georgie said.
"I don't know what to do!"

"Let the dentist pull it out,"
Carol said.

"Oh, no," Georgie said, "I don't want the dentist to pull it!"

"What's wrong?" asked Bobby.

"My tooth is loose," Georgie said.
"I don't know what to do!"

"Twist it!" Bobby said.
"Twist it until it comes out."

"I won't twist it," Georgie said.
"It might bleed!"

"What's wrong?" asked Linda.

"My tooth is loose," Georgie said.
"I don't want a string!
  I don't want an apple!
  I don't want the dentist to pull it!
  And I won't twist it!"

"When my tooth was loose," Linda said, "my grandma gave me fudge. I bit the fudge and swallowed my tooth."

"You swallowed your tooth!" Georgie said.
"I don't want to swallow a tooth.
   It might grow inside me!"

Georgie still didn't know
what to do.

"No string!" he cried.
"No apple!"
"No dentist!"
"No twisting!"
"And no fudge!"

"Mama! Mama!" he cried.
"My tooth is loose!"

"Open your mouth," his mother said,
"so I can look at your tooth."

"You can look, " said Georgie,
"but don't touch!"

"You don't have to do anything,"
  said his mother.
"Your tooth will come out all by itself."

And it did!